W9-CBL-516

IN THE SPRING

BY **CRAIG BROWN**

Greenwillow Books New York

Library of Congress Cataloging-in-Publication Data

Brown, Craig McFarland.
In the spring / by Craig Brown.
p.   cm.
Summary: Spring signals the arrival of many babies, both
animal and human, on the farm.
ISBN 0-688-10983-7 (trade).   ISBN 0-688-10984-5 (lib. bdg.)
[1. Babies—Fiction.   2. Birth—Fiction.
3. Domestic animals—Infancy—Fiction.
4. Spring—Fiction.]   I. Title.
PZ7.B81287In   1994   [E]—dc20   92-17465   CIP   AC

Pastels and pen-and-ink were used for the full-color art.
The text type is Zapf International.

Printed in Singapore by Tien Wah Press   First Edition   10 9 8 7 6 5 4 3 2 1

For Rolland George McFarland

In the spring
the ewe had a lamb,

the cat had kittens,

the cow had a calf,

the sow had piglets,

the
nanny goat had a kid,

the hen had chicks,

the duck had ducklings,

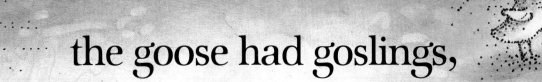

the goose had goslings,

the mare
had a foal,

and the
farmer's wife had twins.

E
BRO   Brown, Craig
          In the spring

$14.00

DATE			
OCT 5 1994			
MAR 2 5 '97			